I need a new bum! Mine's got a **crack**.
I can see in the mirror a crack at the back.

Did I do it on the slide?

Or on the banister inside?

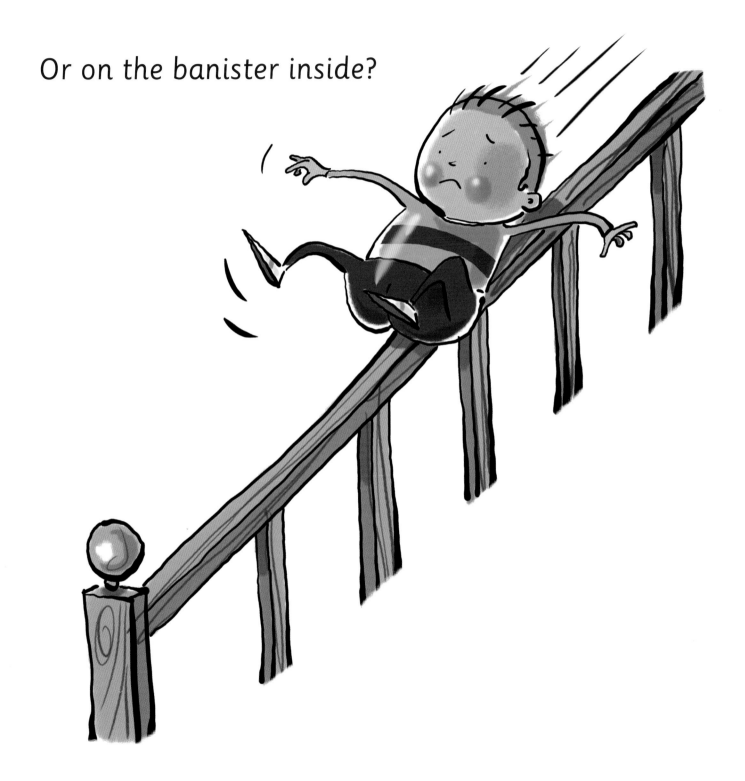

Or when I jumped my BMX?
Or with the fart? That happened next.

Of course! The fart!
That's what blew my bum apart!
Split the thing clean in two.
Now I wonder what to do.

I need a new one.
A green one or a blue one.

A fat one or a thin one.
A wood one or a tin one.

Why not an **arty-farty** bum?
One not to be forgotten,
with watercolours on the top
and a mural on the bottom.

Or ...
yellow spotted?
Purple dotted?

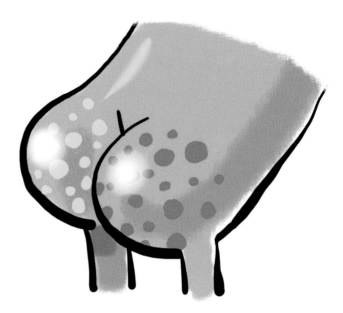

A bum with colour.

A bum with flair.

A bum as **bright** as I dare to wear.
A bum as bright as ...

... Dad's underwear!

Or maybe an alien's bum,
made from a metal
like titanium.

Fireproof!

Bulletproof!

Bombproof!

I'd like a bum that's safety-rated.
The right bum ...

a knight's bum ...
a bum that's **armour-plated**.

What about …
a bum-per?
Chrome?

Why not, I say,
from a 1960s sport coupé,
one made in the USA.

With accessories to complement,
like strips of silver smoothly bent,
a set of lights left and right
for backing round in the night.

Open

With a bumper bum I won't be scared
because bumper cracks can be repaired.

But ...
a bumper bum is huge!
A bumper bum **weighs**
a ton.

I've changed my mind …
I want a lighter one.

A rocket bum?
All **fire** and thrust.

A robo-bum?
Now that bum's a must.

No ... I think it's all too late.
This cracked bum
is my
fate.

I'm here on my own
in this cracked bum zone.
No one to care.
No one to share ...

Wait!
What's that I hear?

This is **outrageous!**
Are bum cracks contagious?

And Dad ...
there's no way of knowing
just how
far
it's
going!

About the author

Hi, I'm Dawn McMillan. I live in a small coastal village on the western side of the Coromandel Peninsula in New Zealand. I live with my husband Derek and our cat, Josie. I write lots of different things: fiction and non-fiction, poetry, stories for school readers and stories for picture books. Sometimes my work is serious, sometimes it's just for fun. Every now and again I write a really crazy story — this is one of those! Enjoy!

About the illustrator

Gidday, I'm Ross Kinnaird. I'm an illustrator and a graphic designer and I live in Auckland, New Zealand. When I'm not illustrating a book, or being cross with my computer, I enjoy most activities to do with the sea. I love visiting schools to talk about books and drawing. (I've been known to draw some really funny cartoons of the teachers!)

First published in 2012 by Oratia Media
This edition published in the UK in 2018 by Scholastic Children's Books
Euston House, 24 Eversholt Street
London NW1 1DB, UK
A division of Scholastic Ltd
www.scholastic.co.uk
London ~ New York ~ Toronto ~ Sydney ~ Auckland
Mexico City ~ New Delhi ~ Hong Kong

Text copyright © Dawn McMillan 2012
Illustrations copyright © Ross Kinnaird 2012
ISBN 978 1407 19601 5

3 5 7 9 8 6 4

The moral rights of Dawn McMillan and Ross Kinnaird have been asserted.

Papers used by Scholastic Children's Books are made from wood grown in sustainable forests.